The DINOSAURS' Night Before CHRISTMAS

By Anne Muecke

Illustrated by Nathan Hale

chronicle books · san francisco

'Twas the night before Christmas, when all through the hall
Not a creature was stirring, there was no sound at all.

OVIRAPTOR

SPINOSAURUS

COMPSOGNATHUS

TYRANNOSAURUS REX

LAMBEOSAURUS

PTERANODON

APATOSAURUS

QUETZACOATLUS

TROODON

SOCKOSAURUS

CORYTHOSAURUS

BRACHIOSAURUS

For Katie, Andrew, and Dave, who fill my life with love, laughter, and great imaginations;
for Eddy, Frank, Samantha, Julia, Liam, Cecilia, Theo, Jane, Jack, and dinosaur lovers everywhere;
and in memory of my beautiful sister Joan, forever my hero.
—A. M.

To Terry Chase and the studio crew.
—N. H.

The songs appearing on the accompanying compact disc have been excerpted from the award-winning CD *Dinosaur Holiday*, created by Museum Music for the American Museum of Natural History, release no. MM140, copyright © 2005 Museum Music, Inc. All rights reserved. Used with permission. Supervising Producer: Joel Goodman; Producers: David M. Somlyo, Dan Rosengard, Anne Muecke, and David Bramfitt. *Dinosaur Holiday* is available from the American Museum of Natural History, www.amnh.org, and Museum Music, www.museummusic.com.

Book design by Katie Jennings.
Typeset in St. Nicholas and Victorian Swash.
The illustrations in this book were rendered in Golden Acrylic on Crescent board.
Manufactured in China

Library of Congress Cataloging-in-Publication Data
Muecke, Anne.
The dinosaurs' night before Christmas / by Anne Muecke ; illustrated by Nathan Hale.
p. cm.
Summary: Every Christmas Eve, the dinosaur fossils in the museum come to life to
sing, dance, eat gingerbread, and celebrate.
ISBN 978-0-8118-6322-3
[1. Stories in rhyme. 2. Dinosaurs—Fiction. 3. Christmas—Fiction. 4. Parties—Fiction.]
I. Hale, Nathan, 1976– ill. II. Moore, Clement Clarke, 1779–1863.
Night before Christmas. III. Title.
PZ8.3.M8675Di 2008
[E]—dc22
2007051277

10 9 8 7 6

Chronicle Books LLC
680 Second Street, San Francisco, California 94107

www.chroniclekids.com

The fossils were standing where they always stood
Looking out o'er a now fast asleep neighborhood;

And across the wide street a small boy,
     tucked in tight,
Wished the museum's dinosaurs
     all a good night.

But just as the boy was beginning to doze,
An unusual clatter of noises arose.
Such a racket of creaking sounds filled the boy's head
That he woke with a start and sat straight up in bed.

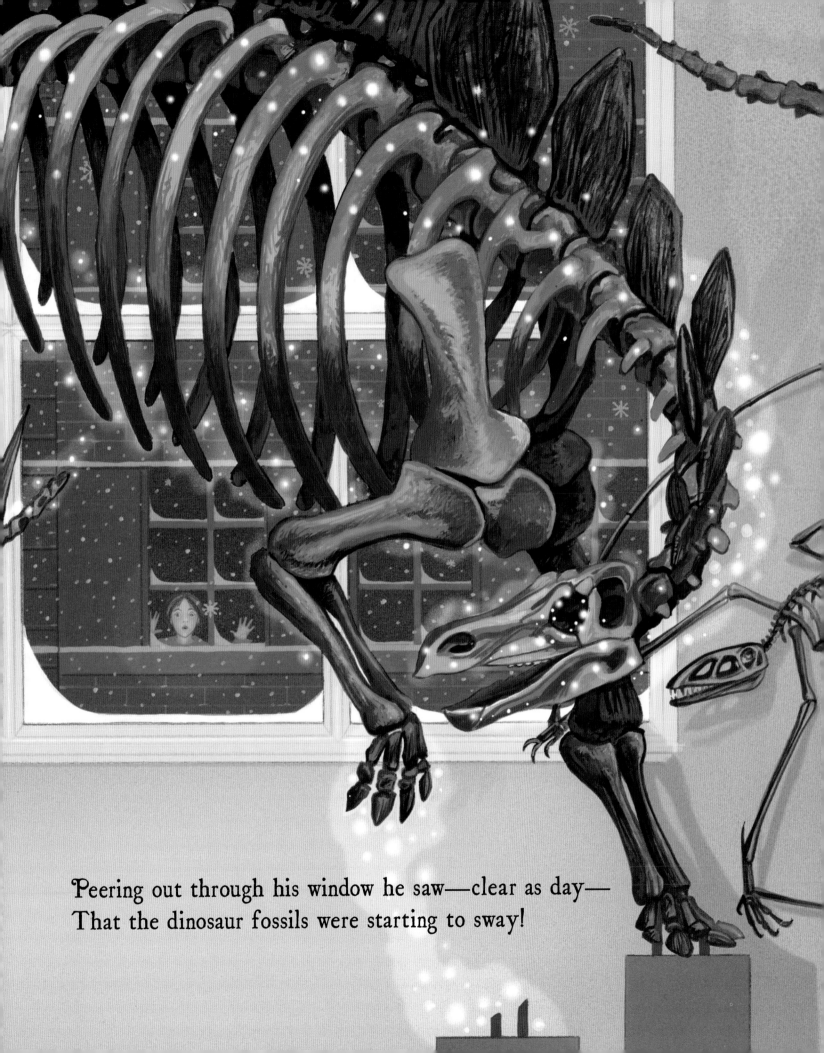

Peering out through his window he saw—clear as day—
That the dinosaur fossils were starting to sway!

Back and forth the bones shook on their pins and their stands,
Swinging necks, bending knees, and outstretching their hands!
And, believe it or not, it was certainly true
That the dinosaurs' bodies were growing anew—
Sprouting rainbows of colorful feathers and scales
From the tops of their heads to the tips of their tails!

So fantastic a scene! The boy had to see more!
So he dashed down the stairs and right out his front door.

With no care about snow drifts that covered the street
The boy hurried across it in just his bare feet!

And, by luck, the boy found the museum unlocked,
So he raced to the dinosaur floor . . .

. . . then he stopped.

For he suddenly thought: "Could a roomful of beasts
Who for millions of years have had nothing to eat
Find a small, bite-sized boy so delicious a sight
That they'd forgo a friendship for sheer appetite?"

And just then from behind the boy came a loud hiss
as a large, toothy mouth seized the boy . . .

. . . with a kiss!

A T. Rex, who was wearing a wreath on his head
Eating handfuls of Pterosaur-shaped gingerbread,
In an ambush had caught the small boy—don't you know?—
Standing right below the dinosaur's mistletoe!

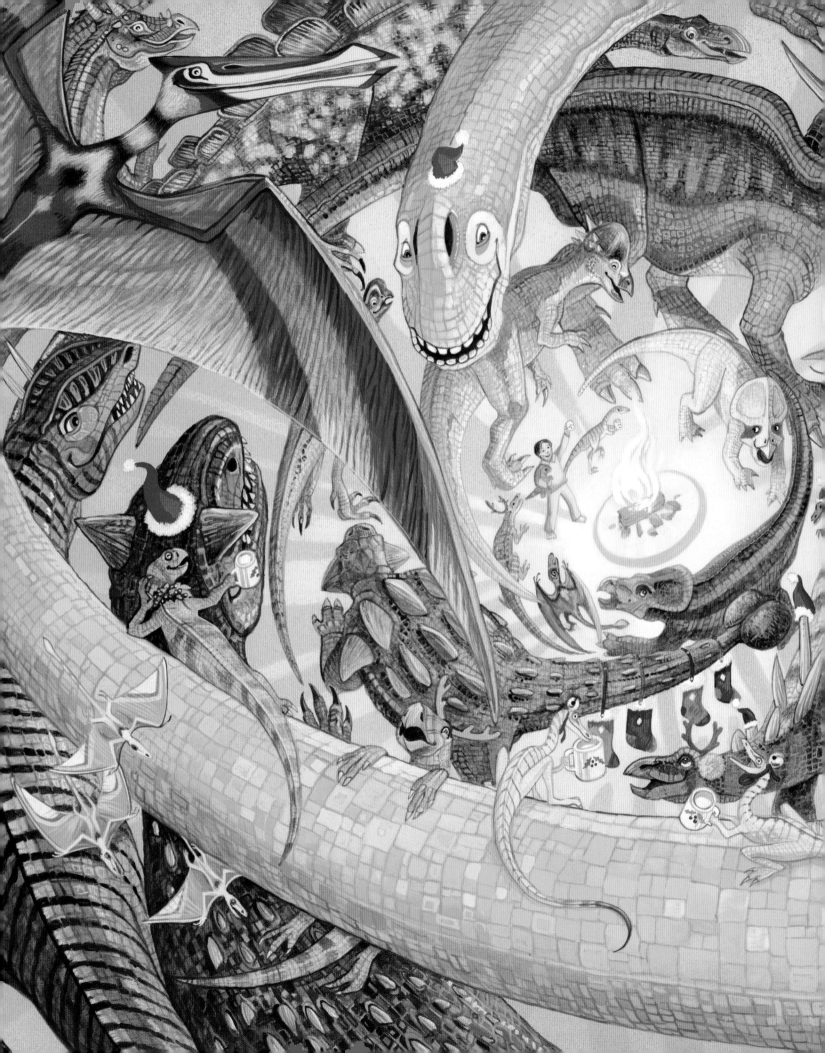

With a pat on the back and a cup of eggnog,
The boy helped the kind dinosaurs light their yule log.
And together they joyfully danced 'round the fire
Singing holiday songs in melodious choir.

Then a band of young duckbills, all dressed up in holly,
Invited the boy, with a gesture quite jolly,
To stand upon their heads and reach way out far
And top their tall tree with a bright Christmas star!

From a distance the soft, tinkling sound of sleigh bells
Echoed through the large hall as a booming voice swelled,
Calling: "Bronto!" and "Maia!" and "Steggie!" and "Packy!"
"On Tri-tops and Raptor! On Rexxie and Bracki!"

And cheers rang out, as through the window appeared
Santasaurus—with sleigh pulled by eight dino-deer!

Handing out gift-wrapped packages to every beast,
Santasaurus swooped down—and then headed due east.
But the boy, catching hold as the sled sailed by . . .

. . . hitched a ride home with Santasaur through the night sky.

Landing safe in his bed
    on soft pillows of down,
The boy waved as the Santasaur
    flew over town,
And the Santasaur said
    as he sped out of sight:
"There's a dinosaur ball
    every Christmas Eve night!"

Shining rays from the morning sun on Christmas day
Made the nighttime festivities fade fast away.
But folks at the museum all wanted to know
Why the T. Rex was holding a sprig of mistletoe.

Dinosaur Christmas Music
and Read-Aloud

The dinosaur-themed Christmas songs on the enclosed CD come
from the award-winning album *Dinosaur Holiday*, produced
by Museum Music with the American Museum of Natural
History. Sing along with the lyrics! The last track on the CD
is a read-aloud of *The Dinosaurs' Night Before Christmas*.

HEY, DUCKBILLS!

Sung to the tune of "Jingle Bells"
Performed by Ann Hampton Callaway

Hey, Duckbills! Hey, Duckbills!
Oh, how can we say
Why your odd-shaped craniums
Evolved to look that way?
Hey, Duckbills! Hey, Duckbills!
Oh, how can we say
Why your odd-shaped craniums
Evolved to look that way?

Dashing looks aside, I think
  that I would dread
To have so many bony pounds
  en-crested on my head!
Unless this crown would bring, along
  with sinus space
Some fine survival advantage to aid my
  humble race!

Oh! Hey, Duckbills! Hey, Duckbills!
Oh, how can we say
Why your odd-shaped craniums
Evolved to look that way?
Hey, Duckbills! Hey, Duckbills!
Oh, how can we say
Why your odd-shaped craniums
Evolved to look that way?

Hidden in your crest were chambers
  full of air.
Could these extra cavities enhance
  your vocal flair?
Did they make your voice resound
  so deep and loud?
Or was your crest just fashion fluff to
  make your mate feel proud?

Oh! Hey, Duckbills! Hey, Duckbills!
Oh, how can we say
Why your odd-shaped craniums
Evolved to look that way?
Hey, Duckbills! Hey, Duckbills!
Oh, how can we say
Why your odd-shaped craniums
Evolved to look that way?

Lyrics by Anne Muecke.
Music Arrangement by David Bramfitt.
Ann Hampton Callaway appears courtesy
of Shanachie Records.

HARK! THE PTERODACTYLS SING

Sung to the tune of "Hark! The Herald Angels Sing"
Performed by Maureen McGovern

Hark! The Pterodactyls sing,
Flying high on reptile wing.
Down below them in a nest
Raptor chicks await breakfast.
Rays of sunshine coax rebirth
From the Mesozoic Earth.
Tiny bug and giant beast
Wake to hunt a new morn's feast.
Hark! The Pterodactyls sing—
Wondering what the day will bring.

Diplodocids in a band
Stroll across the misty land.
Evergreen and fern so sweet
Fuel a thunderous march of feet.
Spindly necks of Seismosaurus
Reach up to the roofs of forests.
Drooping heads of Dryosaurs
Pick new moss from forest floors.
Hark! The Pterodactyls sing—
Wondering what the day will bring.

Rushing through a thicket dense,
A Tyrannosaur, immense
Chases down a hapless prey—
Just in time it gets away!
A voracious appetite

Threatens creatures still in sight.
Silently they crouch and hide
Until T. Rex passes by.
Hark! The Pterodactyls sing—
Wondering what the day will bring.

Deep beneath a rolling sea
Pliosaurs dive gracefully
Searching for a seafood meal—
Trilobite or paleo-eel.
Far below, a shadow, looming—
Suddenly to surface, zooming!
Mouth agape, a Mosasaur
Makes the divers head for shore!
Hark! The Pterodactyls sing—
Wondering what the day will bring.

Mama Raptor has come back
With a tasty morning snack.
Eagerly her hungry brood
Gobble up the baby food.
Far aloft, on graceful wing
Pterosaurs, still hang-gliding,
Herald that the rising sun
Marks another day begun.
Hark! the Pterodactyls sing,
"Day has dawned on everything!"

Lyrics by Anne Muecke.
Music Arrangement by Dan Rosengard.

THE ALLOSAURUS CHORUS

Sung to the tune of the
"Hallelujah Chorus" from Handel's *Messiah*
Performed by The Evergreen Choir, Philip A. Barone, Director

Allosaurus! Allosaurus!
Allosaurus! Allosaurus! Allosaurus!
Allosaurus! Allosaurus!
Allosaurus! Allosaurus! Allosaurus!

For the great Dinosauria reigneth
Barosaurus! Carnotaurus! Hadrosaurus!
  Stegosaurus!
For the great Dinosauria reigneth
Pachysaurus! Maiasaurus! Fabrosaurus!
  Rocasaurus!

For the great Dinosauria reigneth
Gasosaurus! Gryposaurus! Gorgosaurus!
  Gobisaurus!
Longosaurus! Poposaurus! Sellosaurus!
  Technosaurus!
Ultrasaurus! Adasaurus! Dryosaurus!
  Spinosaurus!
Allosaurus! Allosaurus!

The rulers of the paleo world, is become
A kingdom of creatures both big and
  bold—both big and bold,
And they shall roam for millions of years.

Dino kings
For millions of years—Allosaurus!
  No-more-us!
Mighty and strong
For millions of years—Stegosaurus!
  No-more-us!

Dino kings
For millions of years—Hadrosaurus!
  No-more-us!
Mighty and strong
For millions of years—Maiasaurus!
  No-more-us!

Dino kings
For millions of years—Ultrasaurus!
  No-more-us!
Mighty and strong—dino kings—
  mighty and strong

And they shall roam for millions of years.

Dino kings
For millions of years—mighty and strong
Allosaurus! No-more-us!

Their bones preserved for eons and eons and eons.
Fossil kings
For all to see.
Fossil kings
For all to see.
Their bones preserved for eons and eons.
Fossil kings
Preserved in stone.
Pachysaurus! Dryosaurus! Spinosaurus!
  Allosaurus! Allosaurus!

Lyrics by Anne Muecke.
Vocal Arrangement by Philip A. Barone.

DECK THE HALLS WITH STEGOSAURUS

Sung to the tune of "Deck the Halls"
Performed by Donna Murphy

Deck the halls with Stegosaurus,
Fa la la la la la la la la.
Jolly dinos never bore us,
Fa la la la la la la la la.
Go put on your tux or ball gown,
Fa la la la la la la la la.
Dance with Steg and rock
  the hall down!
Fa la la la la la la la la!

Merry Raptors join the party,
Fa la la la la la la la la.
Appetites are big and hearty,
Fa la la la la la la la la.
Games must end in time for dinner,
Fa la la la la la la la la.
Or T. Rex will eat the winner!
Fa la la la la la la la la!

Where's dessert? The guests are
  waiting!
Fa la la la la la la la la.
Eggnog is refrigerating,
Fa la la la la la la la la.

Oh, too bad, the Gobisaurus,
Fa la la la la la la la la.
Ate the cake—there's no more for us!
Fa la la la la la la la la!

Gather round the Songlingornis,
Fa la la la la la la la la.
Strike a merry dino chorus,
Fa la la la la la la la la.
Sing ye loudly, wake the neighbors!
Fa la la la la la la la la.
Calm them down with party favors,
Fa la la la la la la la la.

Stop the music! Stop the jumping!
Fa la la la la la la la la.
Stop the dino-tails-a-thumping!
Fa la la la la la la la la.
Party's over, dawn is breaking
Fa la la la la la la la la.
Just in time, our heads are aching!
Fa la la la la la la la la!

Lyrics by Anne Muecke.
Music Arrangement by David Bramfitt.

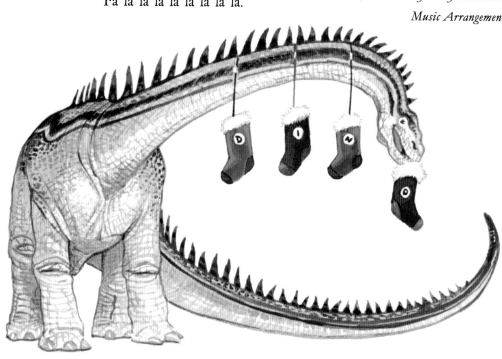

WE WISH YOU A DINO HOLIDAY

Sung to the tune of "We Wish You a Merry Christmas"
Performed by The Evergreen Choir, Philip A. Barone, Director

We wish you a Dino Holiday;
We wish you a Dino Holiday;
We wish you a Dino Holiday;
And a Happy New Year!

Our stockings are hung, our hearts
  filled with glee;
We've wrapped up a Raptor for
  under the tree!

We wish you a Dino Christmas;
We wish you a Dino Christmas;
We wish you a Dino Christmas;
And a Happy New Year!

Eight candles we'll light this
  Hanukkah night;
Dinosaur-a-Menorah will shine
  clear and bright!

We wish you a Dino Hanukkah;
We wish you a Dino Hanukkah;
We wish you a Dino Hanukkah;
And a Happy New Year!

Our kinara is lit, our Kuumba's increased;
We're letting the dinosaurs join
  in the feast!

We wish you a Dino Kwanzaa;
We wish you a Dino Kwanzaa;
We wish you a Dino Kwanzaa;
And a Happy New Year!

We wish you a Dino Holiday;
We wish you a Dino Holiday;
We wish you a Dino Holiday;
And a Happy New Year!

Lyrics by Anne Muecke.
Music Arrangement by Dan Rosengard.

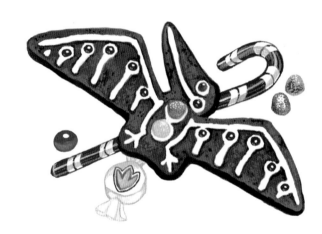

THE DINOSAURS' NIGHT BEFORE CHRISTMAS

Read by Al Roker.
Original Music by David Bramfitt.